To Uli and Christian,
for whom this story was written ~ A. S. & B. R.

For Claire & Ari,
sisters-in and out-of-law ~ S. J.

tiger tales
5 River Road, Suite 128, Wilton, CT 06897
Published in the United States 2016
Originally published in Great Britain 2016
by Little Tiger Press
Text copyright © 2016 Andrea Schomburg and Barbara Röttgen
Illustrations copyright © 2016 Sean Julian
ISBN-13: 978-1-68010-031-0
ISBN-10: 1-68010-031-9
Printed in China
LTP/1400/1429/0216
All rights reserved
10 9 8 7 6 5 4 3 2 1

For more insight and activities, visit us at
www.tigertalesbooks.com

A Friend Like You

by **Andrea Schomburg** *and* **Barbara Röttgen**

Illustrated by **Sean Julian**

tiger tales

Rocky River Public Library

Once more, autumn had come.
Squirrel had been very busy, dashing
up and down the trees. And everywhere
he had buried nuts for the cold
months ahead.

When he was finished,
he sat down to rest.

"Aaaah," he sighed happily.
"All set for winter."

Suddenly, a bird flew down
and landed next to him.

"Where did you come from?"
asked Squirrel.

"A long way from here," said the bird.
"And now I'm tired."

"Have a nut!" said Squirrel.

"Thank you very much!" replied the bird.
"But actually, I only eat worms."

"Why not eat a nut for a change?"
said Squirrel.

"Hmmm, I might give it a try,"
answered the bird,
tasting the nut carefully.

Then he fluffed his feathers
and hopped from
foot to foot.

"Well, what do you know?"
he chirped. "Who would
have thought? Nuts are
delicious!"

"Would you like to come climbing?" asked Squirrel. "I'll show you my favorite tree."

"Actually, I can't really climb," said the bird.

"But you can fly, can't you?" said Squirrel.

"Yes, I can!" replied the bird.

Squirrel darted to the
highest treetop, and
the bird flew with him—
high, high up.

Squirrel turned somersaults
while the bird sat in the top
branch of the tree. He sang
so sweetly that Squirrel
had happy goosebumps
all over his back.

"Come sing with me!"
called the bird.

"Actually, I can't really sing,"
said Squirrel.

"Then why not hum along?"
suggested the bird.

"Well," said Squirrel,
    "I might give it a try!"

The bird sang, and Squirrel hummed along,
    bouncing on the branch with joy.

They played
   and climbed,

and jumped
   and hopped,

and flew, and sprang,
and sang together
all day long.

Then they sat on the grass, eating,
and watching the sunset.

"I'm so happy I met you!"
said the bird.

"I'm happy, too!" nodded Squirrel. "When you sing, it gives me happy goosebumps all over my back. Imagine us meeting like that, out of the blue, and having so much fun together!"

"Yes," agreed the bird. "I never thought I would meet a friend like you."

"You know what?" said Squirrel.
"I've buried so many nuts, more than
enough for two. And there's so much
space in my nest. Would you like to
stay with me?"

"Yes," replied the bird. "I would.
Very much. But . . ."

". . . I can't."

"Why not?"
cried Squirrel.

"It was wonderful spending the day with you,"
said the bird. "But I'm a bird, see?

I can't eat nuts all the time—
I'd miss my worms.

And it makes me so happy to fly.
I'm sorry, but I can't stay."

"But wait!" exclaimed Squirrel.
"You could still eat worms—
and just have nuts
for a change.

"You could fly away whenever you like
and then come back again. There are so many
fun things we could do together!"

The bird thought for a moment.
Then he smiled and said,
"I might give it a try!"

And that's how
Squirrel and the bird stayed together.

And it didn't matter at all that they
were very different.
It was exactly right,
just the way it was.